The Voyage of the Beetle

A Journey around the World with Charles Darwin and the Search for the Solution to the Mystery of Mysteries, as Narrated by Rosie, an Articulate Beetle

Anne H. Weaver
ILLUSTRATED BY George Lawrence

UNIVERSITY OF NEW MEXICO PRESS
Albuquerque

To our children:
Emma Rose, James, and Jessica

ACKNOWLEDGMENTS

Writing *The Voyage of the Beetle* was itself a journey of discovery and delight. Many people contributed to its final incarnation, and we are deeply grateful for their support. Jennifer Owings Dewey brought us together as author and illustrator, encouraged our initial stumbling steps in the world of children's books, and smoothed the path into publication. James Thompson thought that the tale should be told by a beetle. Eva Lawrence, Steve Thompson, Jessica Thompson, and Michele Lis were unwavering in their faith in us and honest in their advice.

Special thanks to Steve Lindsay for his excellent map making assistance. Many thanks to Francis and Mary Louise Nenno and everyone at Discovery Exhibits for gifts of time and support.

We also want to acknowledge Tania Garcia for her creative vision and beautiful book design; and Kristen Bettcher, for her focused commitment and gentle editorial guidance. Finally, we want to thank Luther Wilson and Clark Whitehorn at UNM Press for rescuing the Beetle when it met with rough seas on its voyage to final publication.

Published 2007
Printed in China by Four Colour Imports, Ltd./Everbest

13 12 11 10 09 08 07 1 2 3 4 5 6 7

Library of Congress Cataloging-in-Publication Data

Weaver, Anne H., 1947–
The Voyage of the beetle : a journey around the world with Charles Darwin and the search for the solution to the mystery of mysteries, as narrated by Rosie, an articulate beetle / Anne H. Weaver ; illustrated by George Lawrence.
p. cm.
Includes bibliographical references and index.
ISBN 978-0-8263-4304-8 (cloth : alk. paper)
1. Darwin, Charles, 1809–1882—Juvenile literature. 2. Beagle Expedition (1831–1836)—Juvenile literature. 3. Naturalists—England—Biography—Juvenile literature. I. Lawrence, George, 1953– ill. II. Title.

QH31.D2W43 2007
576.8'2092—dc22

2007008924

"If we could imagine a male [atlas beetle] . . . with its polished bronze coat of mail, and its vast complex horns, magnified to the size of a horse, or even a dog, it would be one of the most imposing animals in the world."

—CHARLES DARWIN

"If a human being were reduced to the size of a beetle, it would make a most tempting and succulent repast for an atlas beetle."

—ROSIE
(*Cetonia aurata*, a rose chafer beetle, companion to Charles Darwin on the voyage of the H.M.S. *Beagle*)

CONTENTS

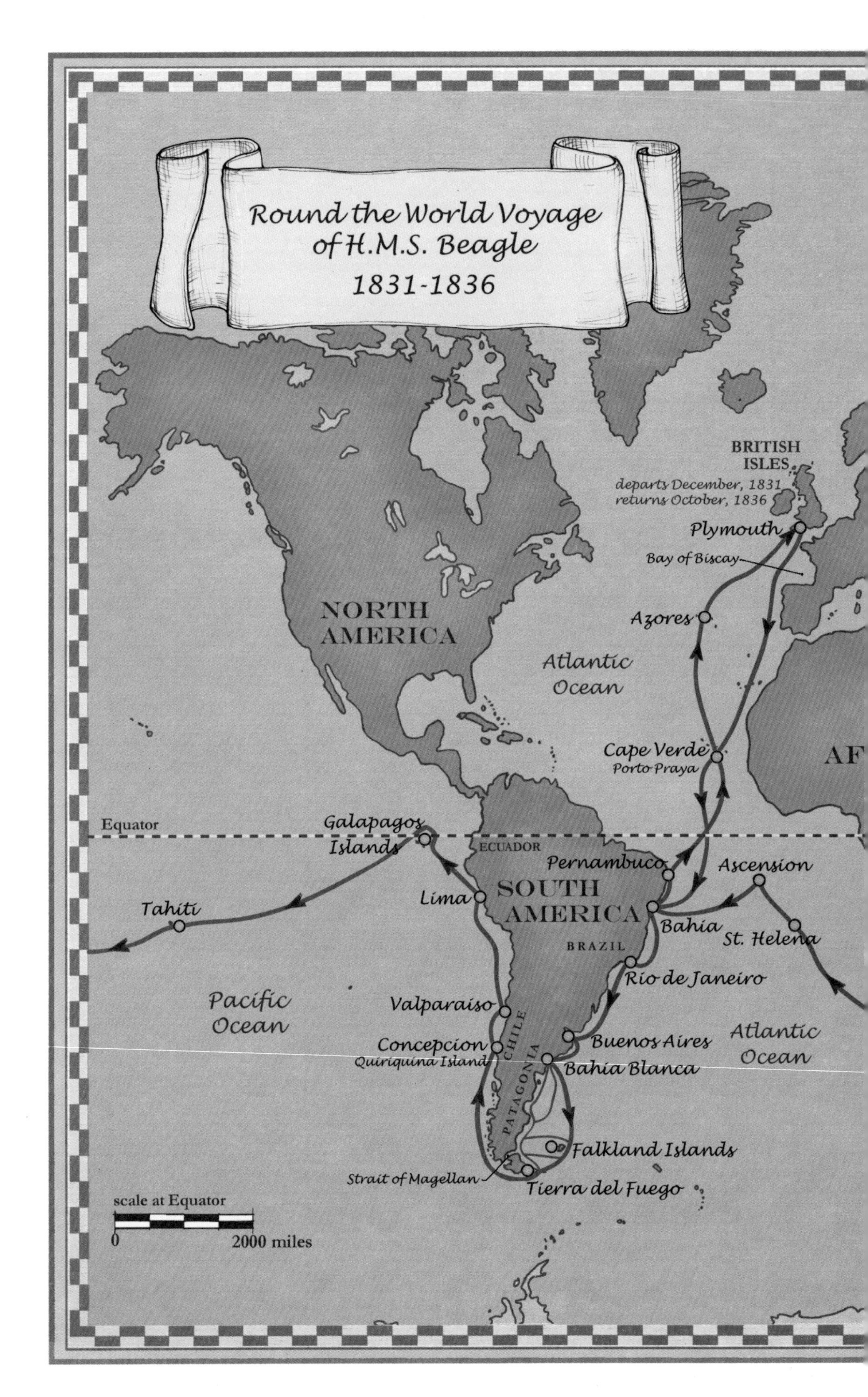
Round the World Voyage of H.M.S. Beagle 1831-1836
BRITISH ISLES
departs December, 1831
returns October, 1836
Plymouth
Bay of Biscay
NORTH AMERICA
Azores
Atlantic Ocean
Cape Verde
Porto Praya
AF
Equator
Galapagos Islands
ECUADOR
Pernambuco
Ascension
Lima
SOUTH AMERICA
Tahiti
Bahia
St. Helena
BRAZIL
Rio de Janeiro
Pacific Ocean
Valparaiso
CHILE
Concepcion
Quiriquina Island
Buenos Aires
Atlantic Ocean
PATAGONIA
Bahia Blanca
Falkland Islands
Strait of Magellan
Tierra del Fuego
scale at Equator
0
2000 miles

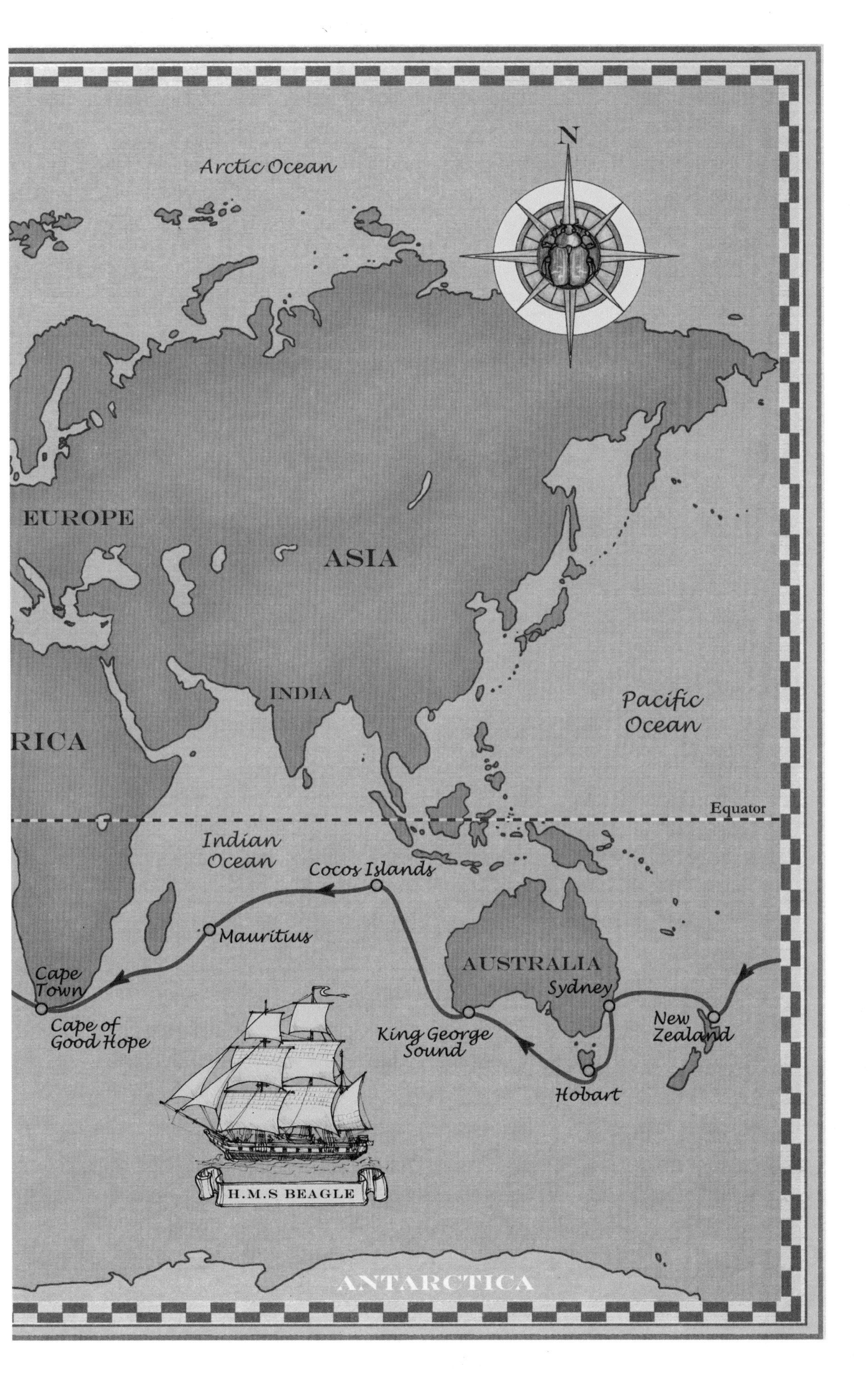

N
Arctic Ocean
EUROPE
ASIA
INDIA
RICA
Pacific Ocean
Equator
Indian Ocean
Cocos Islands
Mauritius
Cape Town
Cape of Good Hope
AUSTRALIA
Sydney
King George Sound
New Zealand
Hobart
H.M.S BEAGLE
ANTARCTICA

CHAPTER 1

The Mystery of Mysteries

Hence, both in space and time, we seem to be brought somewhat near to that great fact—that mystery of mysteries—the first appearance of new beings on this earth.

Charles Darwin, The Voyage of the *Beagle*

Charles Darwin and I first met under a rock. I was dreaming of sweet juicy rosebuds one sunny May morning in 1831, when a rude rustling of leaves and a dazzling shaft of light awakened me. An enormous face, framed by fly-away red hair, loomed above me. An immense hand came down. I struggled, scrambling and squirming, but I could scarcely unfold my wings, and I feared I was lost. An enormous brown eye peered at me through curled fingers.

"What a beautiful specimen of the English *Cetonia aurata,* the rose chafer beetle," murmured the giant who held me, "but—could it be that she's blushing?" I drew myself up with dignity. Really! To imagine I would be flattered at being called "beautiful" by such a large, ungainly two-legged individual! But it was clear that he could recognize beauty when he saw it, and I stopped struggling long enough for mutual introductions.

My captor was a young man named Charles Darwin. Charles later became one of the most well-known scientists in the world. On the morning we met, however, he was still a student at Cambridge University in England. Charles was on his way

to visit his friend and teacher, Professor John Henslow, at the professor's home not far from the university.

Charles was intensely interested in the natural world, and turned out to be a true beetle lover. He was a congenial fellow and charming enough to persuade me to return with him to his student lodgings a few blocks away. Although I loved my quiet home in Professor Henslow's abundant rose garden, I had long felt a very unbeetlelike urge to see more of the world.

My fateful decision to join Charles led to a lifetime of discovery and a long and fruitful friendship. Charles installed me comfortably in his light-filled first-floor rooms in a part of Cambridge University called Christ's College. He called me Rosie, after my fondness for that most elegant and fragrant of flowers. (I preferred to call him by his given name of

Charles rather than his silly nickname of Gas, which came from an unfortunate chemistry experiment in his past.)

Charles was studying theology at Cambridge and planned someday to be a preacher in a country church. This career would give him a secure living and allow him plenty of time to follow his true passion: the investigation of the natural world. Little did he know that he would become famous as one of the greatest naturalists of all time.

Before Charles found me, I had led a typical beetle's life. Like most of my kind, when I was a young larva I was a bit of a loner. As a youngster, I stayed awake late into the night, and spent most of my time looking for something to eat. After my metamorphosis into an adult, I led a more leisurely existence, flirting with eligible young bachelors and dining only on the finest rosebuds and young leaves. I have many fond memories of long evenings spent watching my cousins, the fireflies, put on their brilliant fireworks displays or attending cricket concerts. In the ordinary course of things, I would have laid a clutch of eggs and hatched a family of my own.

Meeting Charles changed all that. If only I had known the wonderful life that lay before me, I would have rushed into Charles's hand when he lifted that rock and disturbed my nap, instead of struggling to escape!

The highlight of our life together was a round-the-world voyage on a British navy ship, the H.M.S. *Beagle*. We spent almost five years on the voyage of the *Beagle,* from December 27, 1831, to October 2, 1836, visiting South America, New Zealand, Australia, Tahiti, and the southern coast of Africa.

Charles was definitely an adventurer. When I say this, I mean it in the regular sense, of course. He exuberantly sought new experiences, from learning to lasso wild cattle, to peering into volcanoes, to venturing deep into the Amazon jungle in search of knowledge. But Charles was another kind of adventurer as well. He was an adventurer in the world of ideas. He had a rare gift for looking at old facts in a new way. In doing so, and in writing about it, he changed our understanding about life on Earth.

Our early months together, before our great voyage, were wonderful, carefree times. During the days, we roamed the fens, woods, and marshes of Cambridgeshire, often in the company of Professor Henslow. We collected curiosities—rocks, plants, and especially insects. Charles would carefully record the day's events and observations in his journal—a habit he kept for his entire life.

We spent our evenings in friendly argument. "Rosie," Charles would say, "isn't it astonishing how every kind, or species, of creature fits into its environment as if it were designed for it? Take beetles like you, for instance. Like others of your kind, you are ideally suited for the life you lead: your mouthparts work perfectly to nip away tough leaf bits, and your antennae are finely sensitive to the smallest changes in odor signals from other beetles. But you are unique as well. Why is no beetle exactly like another? Why are there so many different kinds of beetles? Why are there so many kinds of living things altogether? Where do the different kinds of living things come from?"

I swayed from side to side at the rapid stream of questions. But it was Charles's burning curiosity, his patience in seeking answers, his careful observations, and his faithful record keeping that later led to his great discoveries about what Charles called the "mystery of mysteries":

Why are there so many different kinds, or species, of living things on the Earth, each uniquely fitted for its environment?

Charles was the first person to find a scientific explanation for the mystery of mysteries. Of course, he did have a little help. I hope you won't think me immodest if I say that he could not have solved the mystery without me. We beetles have been around for more than 200 million years, ten times longer than human beings like my friend Charles. We have an ancient and unique vantage point when it comes to understanding the mysteries of nature.

Of course, I had to be tactful, for Charles had a mind of his own and did not always heed my advice. I remember one time when his failure to listen to me left, shall we say, a rather bad taste in his mouth.

We were on a collecting expedition, not long after we met, when Charles spotted an intriguing new beetle emerging from the bark of a tree. Snatching it up, he was about to pop it into a collection bottle when another, even more interesting beetle meandered by. Well, he still had one hand free, so he reached for that one, too. While he was trying to figure out how to save both beetles, he spotted still another beetle crawling up a nearby tree trunk. Two hands, three beetles . . . what to do?

"No, Charles!" I cried, as I realized the solution he had in mind. But I was too late: into his mouth went the second beetle, in order to free his hand to capture beetle Number Three. Number Two was not about to stand for such treatment. (And who could blame him?) "Take that," he shouted, squirting very nasty juice into Charles's mouth. Out he popped, damp but unharmed, and he scurried indignantly away.

Charles was so disappointed, not to mention a bit woozy from his unexpected "refreshment," that I didn't have the heart to mock him, and I doubt that he heard my softly murmured "I told you so."

Charles recovered quickly enough and looked at the whole episode as another example of how well suited living things

are to survival. "That wily creature will doubtless survive to have a clutch of little ones as nasty-tasting as it is," he sighed, with a wryly appreciative smile.

Working with Charles kept me young. And, like a youngster, I was often busy at night. When Charles slept, I would dip a forefoot into Charles's ink bottle and make a few notes of my own. By the glow of moonlight, I recorded details that Charles, as observant as he was, might have missed. Often, I would include a little clue to the mystery of mysteries for Charles to decipher, slipping clues on little scraps of paper between the pages of his diary.

The story that follows comes from these footnotes, and from conversations that Charles and I had as he sought the answer to the mystery of mysteries. In each of the chapters that follow, I have copied my clues for you to read. I suspect that you might be able to solve the mystery even before Charles does.

CHAPTER 2

The *Beagle*

After having been twice driven back by heavy southwestern gales, Her Majesty's ship Beagle, a ten-gun brig, under the command of Captain FitzRoy, R.N., sailed from Devonport on the 27th of December, 1831. The object of the expedition was to complete the survey of Patagonia and Tierra del Fuego . . . to survey the shores of Chile, Peru, and of some islands in the Pacific—and to carry a chain of chronometrical measurements round the World.

Charles Darwin, The Voyage of the *Beagle*

"Ouch and ***!@@$#(*+*)," exclaimed Charles. We had been living aboard the H.M.S. *Beagle*, a British navy sailing ship, for some weeks, but Charles still found it difficult to dress in the tiny space between his hammock and the map table that almost filled our 5-foot (1.5-meter)-high cabin in the stern of the *Beagle*. His elbows were bruised and the top of his head scraped from his daily struggles to pull on the white linen shirts that had been hand sewn for him by his old housekeeper back in England, and his dark blue woolen sea coat.

Despite the irritations of living in the tiny cabin, we were glad to be under way at last. The ship had sat in Plymouth Harbor for long weeks during November and December of 1831, awaiting favorable sailing weather. The *Beagle* was a ten-gun brig belonging to the British Royal Navy. Under the

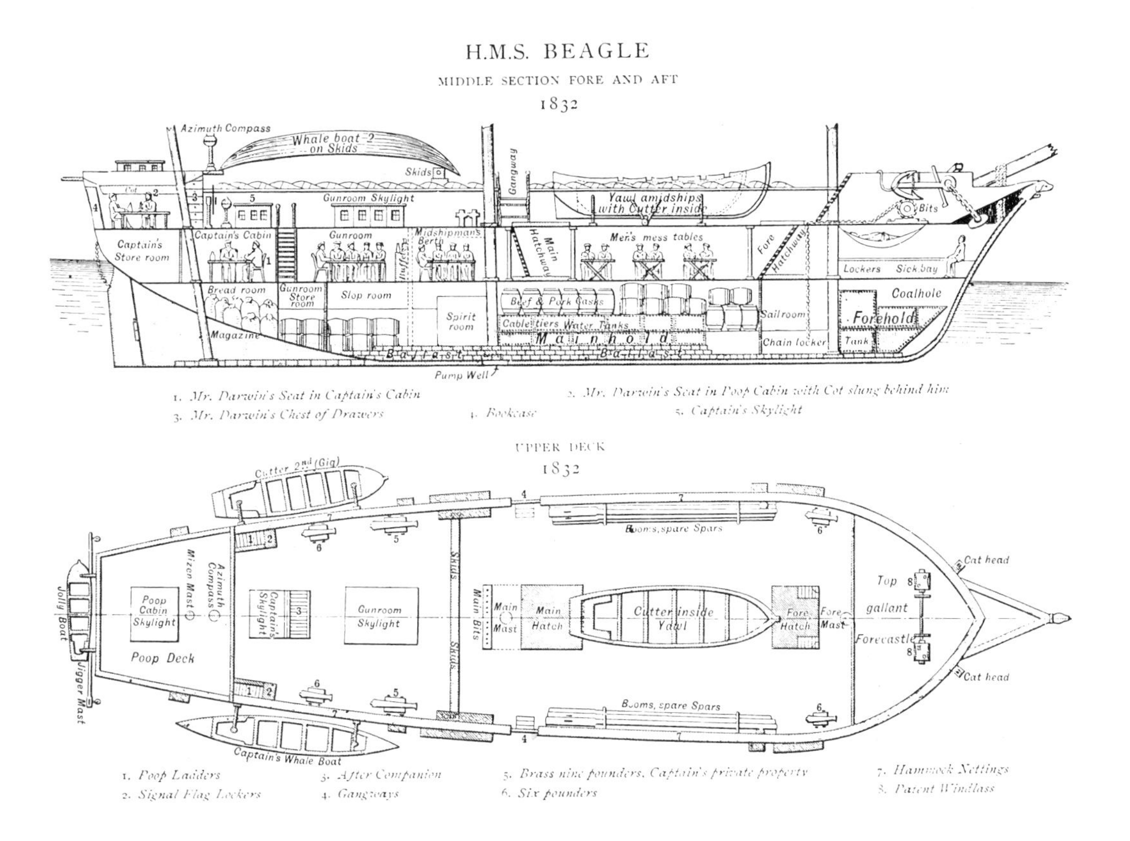

command of Captain Robert FitzRoy, the ship was commissioned to map and describe the coast of South America, including Brazil, Patagonia, Tierra del Fuego, Chile, Peru, and some of the Pacific Islands. The British, determined to be masters of the sea, were looking for suitable ports to dock and take in supplies.

Charles had been invited to be the ship's naturalist—to collect specimens of the plants and animals in the places we visited, and to record descriptions of the geology and natural environment. Because Charles was an educated and cultured young man, Captain FitzRoy had also chosen him to be his dining companion during the long voyage.

Surrounded by fine linen, silver, and crystal, Charles and the captain dined in quiet luxury, conversing about lofty topics. I rarely accompanied Charles to his meals in the captain's cabin. I preferred the boisterous and witty companionship of the ship's officers who dined in the gun room, sharing gossip and tales of adventure at sea. I enjoyed the sense of danger and daring to be found in the presence of the heavy ship's cannons and experienced navy men. (Though, to be sure, in all our time on the *Beagle* we rarely had a chance to fire those huge guns, and then only to greet other ships.)

We had been at sea for several weeks before Charles mastered the art of climbing into his sleeping hammock. I adjusted more easily to my own sleeping arrangements, a dark recess in a drawer. Charles's grunts and complaints reminded me of the first time we inspected the *Beagle*.

"You don't expect me to sleep in that!" I had exclaimed when Charles showed me the hammock that was slung above the map table at night.

"It's easy, Rosie, just watch." Charles tried to reassure me by climbing onto the swinging rope bed. The next second, he was sitting on the deck of the cabin, blinking up at me with surprise. "Er, ahem, let's try that again," he muttered. "Oooooops . . . umph!"

"One more time," he said in a jaunty, if breathless, voice, ignoring the expressions of the experienced sailors who were peering in the door, trying not to chuckle. "Ah, there, simple as can be," he said. He lay there with his knees in the air, his chin cramped against his chest, and his feet pressing on the wall. The tiny cabin, designed to conserve space, offered little room to stretch out. Tall sailors learned to sleep snugly curled up, but Charles despaired at folding his 6-foot (183-centimeter) frame into the short space allowed.

Captain FitzRoy, who was proudly showing us his ship, tactfully concealed a smile as he turned to one of the crew standing by. "Bring the carpenter. We'll need to remove one of the drawers against the wall to make room for Mr. Darwin's feet."

"Whatever happened to the quiet country parish we talked about last year?" I muttered. "I like my bed on solid earth, preferably under a nice cool pile of leaf mold."

Charles laughed at my complaints. "Look, Rosie, when they take out the drawer I'll have room for my feet and you'll have a safe dark corner to sleep in."

"Let's hope you sleep peacefully," I muttered nervously, imagining my lovely yellow-green blood smeared against the wall by a restless foot. It was fortunate for Charles that he did master mounting and emerging from the swinging hammock. Not only did he turn out to be a restless sleeper (I moved my bed to a drawer of the map table), but he was all too often seasick.

Although they are not nearly as colorful as beetles, humans come in an attractive range of colors: creamy beiges, rich browns, delicate pinks, burnished reds, and bronzes. But I had never seen a green human before Charles's first bout of seasickness.

We were three days out of England, approaching the Bay of Biscay, when we hit stormy seas. I woke to find Charles lurching out of his hammock. He hurried to the rail of the ship and launched his dinner into the waves. Leaning his head against the railing, Charles moaned softly. When he looked up, I saw that his face had gained a pale greenish tint. Fascinated, I wanted to get into a serious conversation about color change in humans. I also wanted to know why he spit a perfectly good dinner into the ocean.

Charles's expression warned me that this was not the time for one of our discussions.

"I would never have supposed how miserably ill one could become from the motion of a ship at sea," he moaned.

Just then, Jemmy Button came along. Jemmy was a teenager from Tierra del Fuego, at the tip of South America. Captain FitzRoy had visited Tierra del Fuego on an earlier voyage, and had taken Jemmy and three other native people to England. One of the men died of smallpox in England, but Captain FitzRoy promised to return Jemmy Button (whose Fuegian name was Orundellico), a young man they called York Minster, and an eleven-year-old girl they called Fuegia Basket to their homes and families.

"Poor, poor fellow," Jemmy said in a plaintive voice. "Poor, poor fellow." Then he walked away chuckling. Jemmy, like most native people from Tierra del Fuego, spent much of his life fishing for his supper from small canoes in the ocean, and he couldn't understand the idea of anyone's being made ill by the motion of a boat.

Charles spent many seasick days tossing in his hammock. He managed to survive on a diet of biscuits, raisins, hot wine, and a rubbery-tasting broth made of sago flour by the ship's doctor, Mr. Bynoe.

Charles's illness and inability to work made him a restless

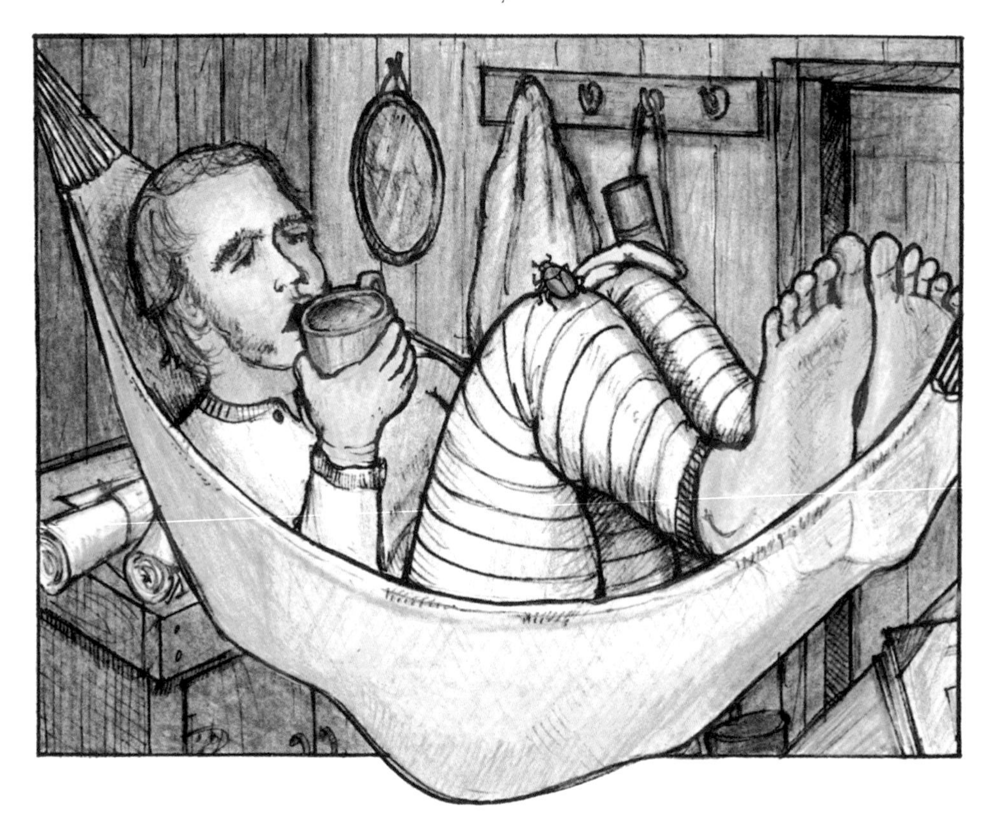

and irritable cabin mate. I found myself wandering about the ship in search of more cheerful companionship. This I found in a fellow adventurer, a brightly colored cricket named Motley. Motley had been blown almost 400 miles (644 kilometers) from Africa and had stopped to rest in the *Beagle*'s rigging. Although, like many inhabitants of the tropics, he looked rather gaudy, my well-traveled new friend had engaging stories to tell, and his music harmonized beautifully with the flutes and fiddles brought out by the crew to pass the evening hours.

Motley was not my only insect companion, for even when we were far out to sea, many beetles, butterflies, and even spiders floated or flew far from land to alight on the *Beagle*.

By mid-January, after sailing south for three weeks, we found ourselves in warmer, calmer water. Charles busied himself by designing and supervising the construction of a woolen bag stretched across a bentwood frame. With the help of the ship's carpenter, Mr. Mays, and the sail maker, Mr. Harper, Charles soon had a plankton net that he could draw along the surface of the water in the wake of the *Beagle*, to capture the small plants and animals floating and swimming near the ocean's surface. Charles became so engrossed by the harvest of his net that he no longer dreaded the six weeks it would take to reach the coast of Brazil.

Every day, Charles would examine a fresh catch from the plankton net under a microscope set up on the map table in his cabin. I crawled up to peer through the lens myself when he leaned back to rest his eyes. The microscope revealed a universe of exquisite, rainbow-hued living forms floating in every drop of seawater—each one unique. "How could such beauty be created where no one can see it? These life forms seem destined only to be fish food," Charles murmured. "No two individuals are alike, even within the same species."

Charles's wonderment was the occasion for me to offer the first clue to the mystery of mysteries.

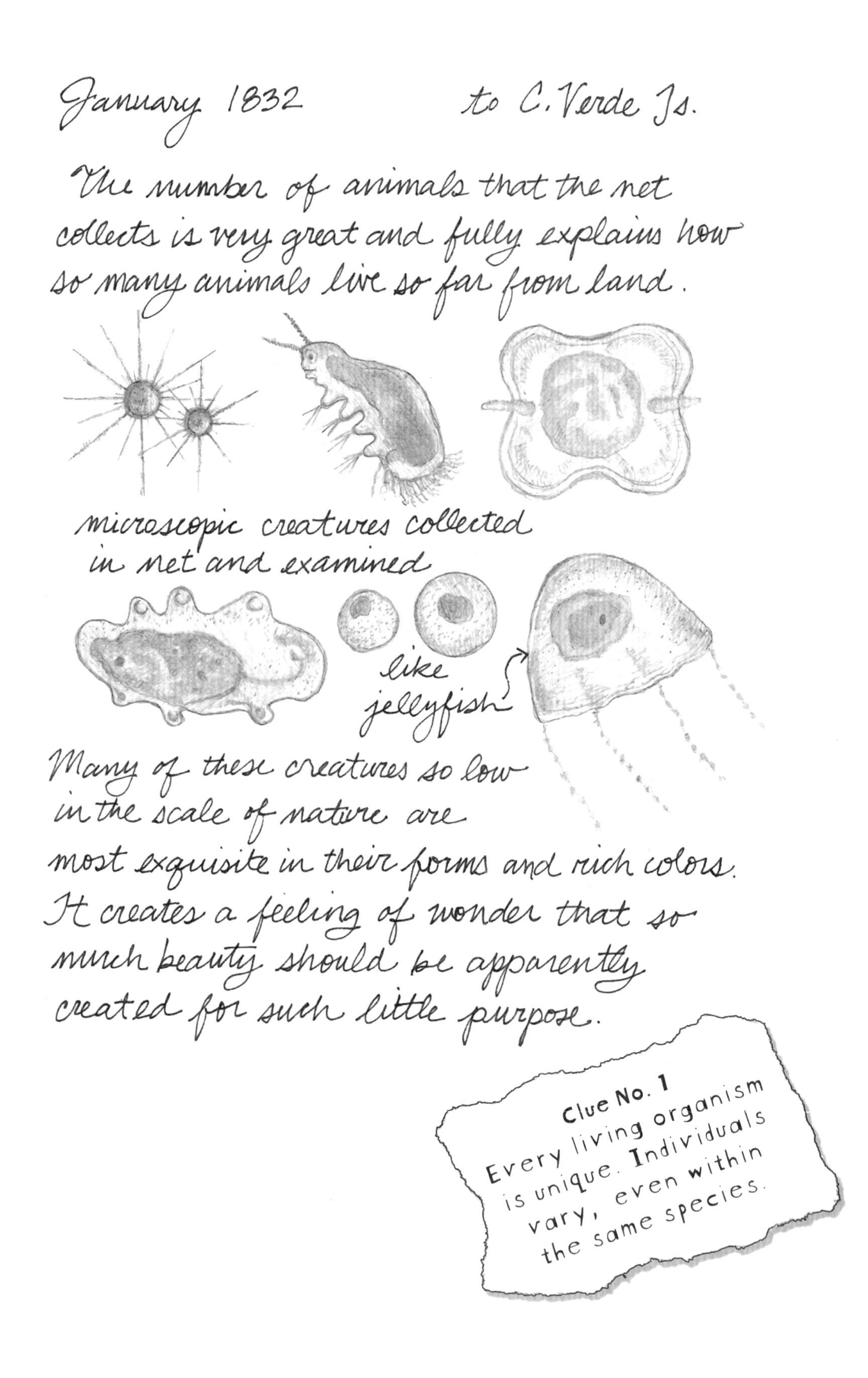
January 1832
to C. Verde Is.
The number of animals that the net collects is very great and fully explains how so many animals live so far from land.
microscopic creatures collected in net and examined
like jellyfish
Many of these creatures so low in the scale of nature are most exquisite in their forms and rich colors. It creates a feeling of wonder that so much beauty should be apparently created for such little purpose.
Clue No. 1
Every living organism is unique. Individuals vary, even within the same species.

Fortunately for Charles's stomach, once we reached South America in late February, our time at sea was punctuated by long weeks when the *Beagle* remained at anchor along the coast. During these intervals, the ship's crew mapped coastal features, describing harbors and hazards future sailors might encounter. Charles would set out on foot or horseback to explore inland, his canvas canteen and leather pouch hanging from his shoulders; his pockets bulging with hammer, bug net, compass, barometer, small telescope, notebook, and collecting bottles.

It was during one of these stops, when the *Beagle* was anchored off the coast of Brazil, that we encountered yet another clue to the mystery of mysteries.

CHAPTER 3

The Brazilian Rain Forest

It is easy to specify the individual objects of admiration in these grand scenes; but it is not possible to give an adequate idea of the higher feelings of wonder, astonishment, and devotion, which fill and elevate the mind.

Charles Darwin, The Voyage of the *Beagle*

"He is truly mad," I muttered as I watched Charles cavorting rapturously through the jungle, talking to himself. His excited movements gave new meaning to the words "leap year," for it was February 29, 1832, and Charles could not contain his exuberance.

For Charles, encountering the Brazilian rain forest for the first time was fulfilling a lifelong dream. I watched him chase a gaudy butterfly, then stop suddenly to gaze for a moment at a strange tree, then turn his attention to a bright fruit, an insect, an orchid.

"How can I ever find words to describe such beauty?" he exclaimed in wonder as he paused to take a breath. "Look, Rosie, at the fireflies. They are brighter, I think, than the fireflies of England." He leaped up again to search for their larvae, which also glowed, but more faintly than their parents. When he touched one, it ceased to glow, feigning death. "Clever cousin," I thought (for fireflies and their offspring, the glowworms, are beetles as well). Charles collected some of the larvae to bring back to the ship.

Surrounded by grasses, brilliant blossoms, green twining vines, and animals crawling, scurrying, flying, and feeding, Charles returned to the ship reluctantly, as a drenching rain began to fall.

When we returned to the *Beagle*, anchored at the port of Bahia, Brazil, Charles placed the larvae he had collected in a box on the map table, supplied them with raw meat, and set me to baby-sitting. I never tired of watching them. Their tails were particularly fascinating—they acted as suckers, by which they could attach themselves to the sides of the box, and they also held drops of digestive fluid. The larvae would bring their tails around to a piece of meat they held in their mouths. They would deposit a drop of digestive fluid on it to dissolve the food before devouring it. I became quite fond of them, though they were a bit clumsy and didn't seem to think of much but their next meal.

These were not the only beetles that we discovered on our voyage. Of the hundreds of thousands of beetles in the world, the beetles of South America are among the most beautiful and strange. And I'm proud to say that everywhere beetles are found, they make an important contribution to the life around them.

I remember one remarkable beetle in particular, a luminous beetle with the rather stodgy name of *Pyrophorus luminosus*. In his behavior, he was anything but stodgy. This fellow, whom we met in Bahia, permitted us to call him Pyro for short.

Of all the members of his species that Charles and I had encountered, Pyro caught our attention because of his particularly well-developed agility. Other *Pyrophorus luminosus* beetles were able to perform acrobatic flips, but Pyro could jump so high that we almost lost him. We found him again only when we heard him call to us from behind a large fern.

Pyro demonstrated a series of marvelous acrobatic tricks for Charles one day. "What awesome springing powers," Charles said admiringly. He would turn Pyro over onto his back. Pyro would bend his head and thorax backward until he rested on the ends of his head and wing cases. Then, releasing his muscles, his body recoiled like a spring, lifting into the air and landing on his feet. Pyro's tricks were actually important to his survival: unlike many insects, he was always able to right himself if overturned, and he was able to spring out of the range of predators when in danger.

Pyro provided an important clue to the mystery of mysteries:

February 1832 Bahia

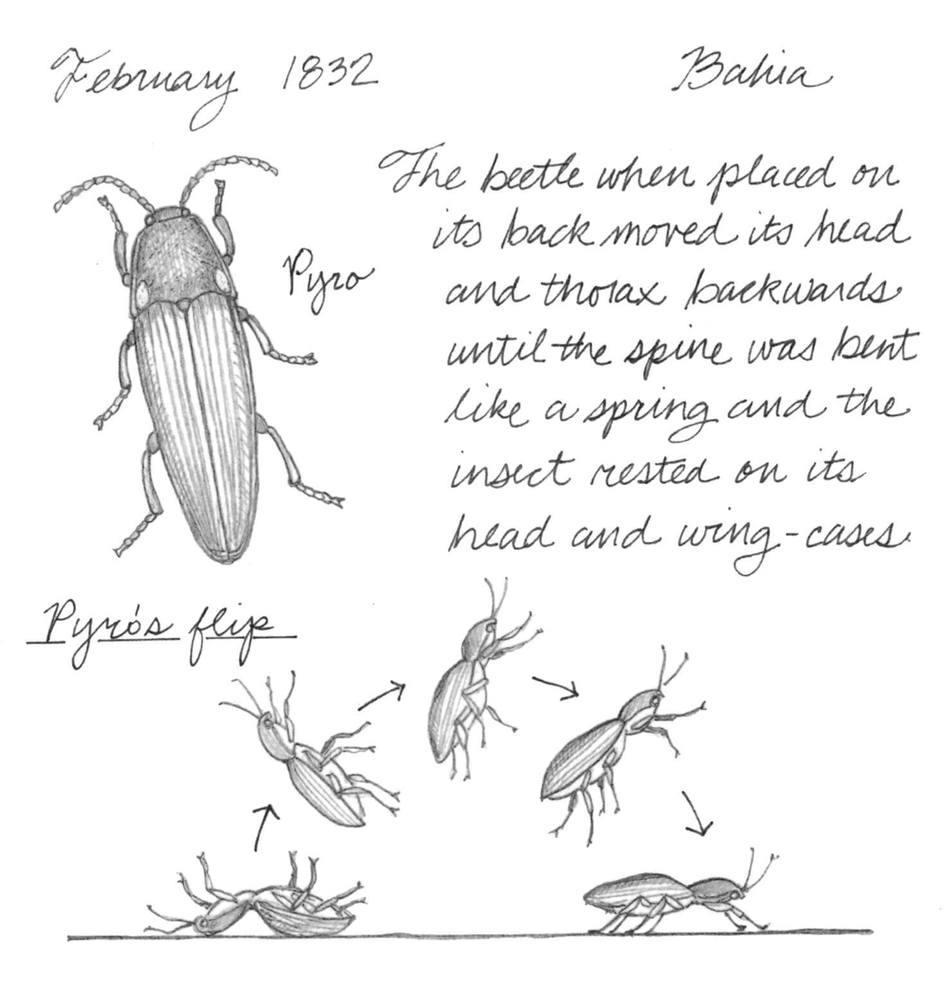

The beetle when placed on its back moved its head and thorax backwards until the spine was bent like a spring and the insect rested on its head and wing-cases.

The effort being suddenly relaxed, the head and thorax flew up, and the base wing-cases struck the supporting surface with such force that the insect was jerked upward to a height of one or two inches.

Clue No. 2

Living things have special traits that enable them to survive in their own particular surroundings. Within a species, some individuals may have a version of the trait that is more helpful to survival than other versions.

One of the most important jobs of beetles is to help sustain life. One of them told us about her work one day as we were walking through the rain forest. Charles had found a wonderfully fragrant fungus and was carrying it back to our camp. (Well, to be accurate, I thought the fungus smelled and tasted like ambrosia; Charles called its fragrance "odious.") Attracted by the odor, a *Strongylus* beetle alighted on the fungus and began to munch delightedly. She was hardly willing to interrupt her meal to talk to me, but when I told her about the mystery of mysteries, she was intrigued.

"You can call me Lulu," she offered. "My family's job is to help make soil from certain fungi that live in the rain forest," she continued. "The fungi feed on fallen leaves, breaking the leaves down into soil that nourishes the trees. We beetles spread the spores of the fungi to fresh piles of leaves. We also participate in the cycle of life-from-death by eating the fungi and turning *them* into soil as well."

Lulu continued, "Our small size and modest coloring help us hide from birds, rodents, and lizards that prey upon us. But not far from here you'll find some really nasty beetles—gaudy, arrogant, vicious creatures who will make a meal of anything that moves, including their smaller relatives like me."

Lulu shuddered, then sighed, "Well, it takes all kinds, I suppose. Just as we control the fungi, the carnivorous beetles keep our population in balance. Otherwise, the whole forest might be overrun and eaten by one kind of creature or another."

I looked up from my conversation with Lulu to see Charles gazing into the distance, lost in thought. I found out why when I read his journal notes that night. There are certain beetles that enjoy an "odious" fungus in England. The English fungus and beetles are both quite different from the South American ones, but they do the same kind of work in both places.

Lulu had provided us with another important clue:

Clue No. 3

In any given environment, each living thing has a special role to play in the intricate cycle of life. In different places, similar functions in the cycle of life are carried on by different organisms.

March 1832 Bahia

Fungus beetle observed in rain forest near Bahia - attracted to a foul smelling fungus which I carried in my hand.

yellow band with black spots

dark red

black

English fungus beetle (drawn from memory) - also feeds on forest floor fungus

red with black spots

We here see in two different countries a similar relation between plants and insects of the same families though the species are both different.

We had many more enjoyable encounters with the diverse kinds of beetles, crickets, butterflies, ants, birds, monkeys, and hundreds of other living organisms that live in the rain forest outside of the port of Bahia.

In mid-March, the *Beagle* sailed south to Rio de Janeiro, Brazil. We arrived at Rio de Janeiro on April 4. While the ship's crew worked at charting this part of the coast, Charles arranged to join a party of riders who were traveling by horse through the wilds of Brazil. During this two-week trip, Charles was often enraptured by the beauty of the forest, teeming with lush trees, swaying ferns, elegant vines, fragrant orchids, and bright birds. He was less enchanted by the sullen hospitality at the coffee, sugarcane, and mandioca plantations where we lodged along the way, and he was much grieved by the misery of the black slaves who worked the plantations.

"Rosie," he confided, "this morning when speaking to one of the slaves, a strong, powerful man, I raised my hands to make my point clearer. He flinched away as if he expected me to strike him. I have never felt so ashamed of humankind, that this man should feel so threatened by an innocent gesture because he has been treated so badly by his fellow humans." The cruelty of one member of the human species to another was a mystery that even Charles could not fathom.

The *Beagle* left Brazil in July of 1832, continuing to map the eastern coast of South America. For many months we traced the coastal features of Uruguay and Argentina. In January of 1833, York Minster, Fuegia Basket, and Jemmy Button were settled at Woollya Sound in Tierra del Fuego, Argentina, along with an English missionary, Mr. Matthews, who hoped to convert the Fuegians to Christianity. I often thought of them in later years, wondering how their lives unfolded after their unexpected journey into another country.

In March of 1833, the *Beagle* visited the Falkland Islands, then headed north again, retracing parts of its journey along the South American coast.

CHAPTER 4

Luck and Long Life

We do not steadily bear in mind, how profoundly ignorant we are of the conditions of existence of every animal; nor do we always remember, that some check is constantly preventing the too-rapid increase of every organized being left in a state of nature. . . . No fallacy is more common with naturalists, than that the numbers of an individual species depend on its powers of propagation.

Charles Darwin, The Voyage of the *Beagle*

On a windy day in April of 1833, I found myself peering over the edge of a rough stone by the side of a deep tide pool. The *Beagle* was exploring the coast of Patagonia, in southern Argentina, and in the meantime we were investigating a desolate rocky beach. I was entranced at the spiraling string of pearls glistening in the April sun near the surface of the tide pool.

Charles's eyes, too, were caught by the double ribbon of beads, which gently rose and fell with the motion of the water. "Oh," he said. "For a moment I thought there were pearls in the water—but those are really hundreds of thousands of sea slug eggs."

There was no need for Charles to know that I, too, had been fooled by the rows of egg cases. I responded with a question to distract him: "But where are the adult sea slugs?"

Charles lifted one rock after another. "Rosie, by my estimate,

there must be six hundred thousand eggs here, but I have found only seven that grew into adults. The pool should be filled with sea slugs. Something must be preventing them from growing up." He sat down to consider the problem.

I offered an idea. "Well, if the pool were full of sea slug hatchlings, what would they all eat? They would soon starve, except for a lucky few who were especially quick at grabbing a meal."

"Yes," mused Charles, "and if there were so many young sea slugs, such a mass would attract flocks of seabirds that love to eat them, and soon there would be only a few left—perhaps those that had the instinct to hide under the rocks, or whose coloring made them more difficult to see."

I reminded Charles how difficult life is in the wild, and he knew it was no different for sea slugs than for birds or rabbits or even beetles, for that matter. "There would be relentless competition, until soon only the quickest, strongest, best at hiding or fighting for food would remain."

I will confess to a certain fondness for sea slugs. Not only do they lay beautiful, shimmering ribbons of eggs, but they are often beautifully colored, with flamboyant names to match their looks—Spanish shawl, white doris, clown. They, like me, are creatures without backbones—or bones of any kind, for that matter. They don't really have brains, either—only a very primitive network of nerves throughout their bodies—yet they are quite capable of finding food in changing water conditions and meandering over the unpredictable, rocky seafloor. Some are able to squirt purple ink at their enemies; others shed their gills if caught by an enemy, slipping away to grow new ones.

Charles was still muttering about sea slugs the next day after pondering their existence all night. "What if predators ate every sea slug before the sea slugs could lay more eggs?" he mused. He immediately answered his own question: "They would all die—they would become extinct." He continued talking to himself: "But what if just a few were able to hide because they were quicker at squirting ink, or because their coloring matched the rocks or kelp where they lived? . . . As the survivors, they would be the ones who laid eggs in the future. The offspring that inherited the same protective coloring or ink-squirting ability would be better survivors, too, and live to have more offspring themselves."

Charles was ready for another clue—he had practically figured this one out for himself.

By the time the *Beagle* started north again, we were more than ready to leave the arid plains and freezing winds of Patagonia behind us.

April 1833 Coast of Patagonia

What variations would enable some sea slugs to survive while others perish?

predator bird

strands of sea slug eggs

tidal pool

A

B

C

slug 'A' has ability to hide in rock crevices

'C' can squirt ink to distract and deter predator

'B' has mottled pattern which blends with sandy bottom of pool

adult white doris sea slug

only seven adults in a pool which contains more than 600,000 eggs

white with black spots

golden yellow gills

Clue No. 4

The individuals that are best able to compete in the struggle for life pass on their survival abilities to their offspring. Individuals that are less able to compete often die before they have offspring. Soon, the only individuals left are those that have inherited the ability to compete most effectively for food or space or safety.

CHAPTER 5

Clues from the Dead

This wonderful relationship in the same continent between the dead and the living, will, I do not doubt, hereafter throw more light on the appearance of organic beings on our earth, and their disappearance from it, than any other class of facts.

Charles Darwin, The Voyage of the *Beagle*

Charles blinked in astonishment as laughter broke out around him. I had to chuckle myself, for Charles had just succeeded in roping his own horse with a set of bolas—leather-covered stone balls joined by a braided leather cord, used for capturing game.

While the *Beagle* surveyed the coast of Argentina in August of 1833, Charles had joined a company of gaucho soldiers to ride from the mouth of the Rio Negro to the port town of Bahia Blanca. Charles planned to meet the *Beagle* at Bahia Blanca in a few weeks. He admired the good manners and hospitality of the tall, handsome gauchos. They took a liking to him, as well, sharing their meals of ostrich dumplings and armadillo steaks, and teaching him to use the bolas.

This morning Charles had been practicing. One of the balls caught on a bush and the other wound around his horse's legs. Fortunately, the horse knew what to do and remained still, so he did not tumble over onto his side. "We have seen every kind of animal caught with the bolas," the gauchos roared, "but never have we seen a man caught by himself!"

Charles continued to record his observations about the people, plants, and animals we encountered. The next clue to the mystery of mysteries, however, came not from living organisms, but from the remains of dead ones, buried in a cliff near Punta Alta, a few miles from the coast.

"Are we almost there?" I gasped. Charles, bent under the weight of a giant leg bone, only grunted a breathless reply. We had found the fossil remains of a strange animal protruding from the cliff. Digging carefully around them, we managed to free several of the bones and were carrying them one by one back to the *Beagle.* Charles would pack them carefully and ship them back to scientists in England.

We paused to take a breath. Standing back from the enormous leg bone, Charles shook his head in amazement. "This animal must have been almost as large as an elephant—but quite different in shape," he mused. "I wonder if anything like it has ever been found before."

We later learned that the leg bone we were carrying belonged to a Megatherium, a giant sloth that lived in North and South America tens of thousands of years ago. Unlike the much smaller tree sloths that live in South America today, the Megatherium lived on the ground, eating leaves and bark stripped from low-growing trees by its sharp claws and rodentlike teeth.

Besides the giant ground sloths, there were long-dead, huge armadillo-like animals and an enormous beast with a long neck like a camel, called Macrauchenia, which resembled the modern llama.

Some of the strangest fossil bones we found belonged to a Toxodon, an ancient animal that was as large as an elephant, with teeth like a beaver, and that had eyes, ears, and nostrils near the top of its skull, like an aquatic creature. "This huge creature must have been almost as bizarre looking as you are, Rosie," he joked. I was not amused. "Look who's talking," I muttered, "a soft-skinned, knobby bag of bones."

Charles examined the red soil clinging to the fossils. "From the way the gravel and mud are found in layers in the cliffside, I believe this soil was part of the bottom of an ancient lake or ocean. When we get back to the ship, Rosie, we'll examine this dirt through the microscope, to discover what tiny animals may have lived in it."

We found the soil to be full of the skeletons of tiny animals, mostly freshwater creatures but some saltwater ones as well, like the ones we had brought up in the plankton net.

"What a strange mixture of life forms," Charles exclaimed.

"The cliff where we found them must once have been the site of a long-ago estuary, where a river met the ocean, mixing the salt water with the fresh."

Still trying to imagine what the coast had looked like in the distant past, Charles continued, "Rosie, the cliff holding the fossils is formed like a gigantic layer cake," he mused. "There are layers of reddish mud and, between them, layers of gravel and shells, just like you see on a rocky beach today. But the cliff is high above the level of the water."

He continued, "Today this area has little vegetation. But there must have been many plants here to support the life of the huge plant-eating Megatherium and other animals we found. What great natural forces must have lifted up the old seashore, caused a river to disappear, and changed even the kinds of plant and animal communities that can live here!"

Charles better understood how the Earth rises and falls many months later, when he witnessed the results of an earthquake in Chile—a story for a later chapter. For the moment, Charles was more worried about Captain FitzRoy's reaction to yet another load of "rubbish" cluttering the *Beagle*'s polished decks. This did not dampen Charles's curiosity, however.

Although many of the animals we found resembled some of the present-day animals of South America, all of them are extinct: the Megatherium, Macrauchenia, Toxodon, and giant armadillos no longer exist except as fossilized skeletons.

I swept my gaze over the expanse of sand, the tall cliffs rising steeply away from the shore. I imagined how it must have looked long, long ago, with gigantic sloths, stubby-legged horses grazing along a river's edge, and huge Toxodons, like deformed hippopotami, munching on the woody bark of shoreline trees.

"From what I have read," he said, "the odd creatures of Australia closely resemble fossils that have been found there, just as the living animals of South America look like the fossils we have discovered here. And the fossils found in Africa are more similar to present-day African animals than they are to South American or Australian fossils."

"He's found another clue, if only he would realize it," I thought. That evening, I inscribed another clue in Charles's diary.

August 1833 Punta Alta

We have found fossilized skeletons of gigantic land animals, each of which resembles a much smaller animal of present day South America

Megatherium

size of elephant

present day sloth

present day capybara

Toxodon

Macrauchenia

size of camel

present day llama

Clue No. 5

New species appear and old ones disappear as the Earth changes. Many of these extinct organisms resemble the ones now living in the same part of the world.

The next day, I felt that my hard work leaving clues at night had paid off, as Charles continued to think about the fossils we found. "It is as if the living animals on each continent are somehow more closely related to past animals on the same continent than they are to animals from distant places today," he observed. "Is it possible that the living animals of today are the descendants of the ones in the past?"

By the time we left Bahia Blanca, we were both ready for new sights; but Captain FitzRoy was determined to have perfect charts. We spent the winter sailing into and out of the coves and inlets of Argentina, Patagonia, and Tierra del Fuego, making sure our previous observations were absolutely correct.

After weeks of enduring bitter stormy weather, we finally sailed through the treacherous Strait of Magellan in early June of 1834. We spent most of that year exploring the coast of Chile and its many coastal islands. The calm waters and warm climate off the central Chilean coast restored our good cheer. But we were shocked out of our peaceful state of mind when we witnessed the effects of a terrible earthquake that hit Chile in late February of 1835.

CHAPTER 6

The Endless Cycle of Change

Daily it is forced home on the mind of the geologist, that nothing, not even the wind that blows, is so unstable as the level of the crust of this earth.

Charles Darwin, The Voyage of the *Beagle*

"Such devastation!" Charles gasped, gazing in horror upon the piles of lumber and furniture, even whole cottage roofs, strewn along the beach.

We had just landed on the island of Quiriquina, off the coast of Chile.

The *mayordomo* of the coastal village of Concepción met us to tell us the terrible news. An earthquake and a tidal wave had ripped through the island two weeks previously. Seventy of the island's villages, including Concepción, had been destroyed in minutes.

We walked along the shore. Huge rock fragments with deep-sea life still clinging to them were flung high onto the beach.

Deep cracks nearly a yard wide had opened up along the cliffs. In some places, the cliffs collapsed into massive piles of rock fragments.

The mayordomo told us that he was on horseback during the quake. Both he and his horse were thrown upon the ground. Seventy cattle standing on a hillside were washed into the sea and drowned. A four-ton cannon was tossed about by the waves. A schooner was left stranded 200 yards (183 meters) inland from the beach.

The heaving force of the earthquake had lifted portions of the coast itself by several feet. Along the new shoreline were masses of dying shellfish that had formerly lain under shallow water.

We gave what help we could to the victims. It was not until very late that night that Charles had time to reflect upon the disaster.

"Rosie, this reminds me of the shoreline at Valparaiso in Chile, where we saw seashells at a height of 1,300 feet [396 meters] above the coast. They must have been lifted up by a series of earthquakes such as we have seen here at Quiriquina. It must have taken a very long time and many, many quakes to lift the land so high above sea level."

The coast here reminded me also of the fossil cliffs at Punta Alta and other parts of the Patagonia coastline. There we had followed an ancient, raised seabed many layers deep along the shore for hundreds of miles. In places, the chalky layers, which contained gigantic oyster shells and tiny marine shells, were over 800 feet (244 meters) thick! A 50-foot (15-meter) layer of rounded gravel topped the old seabed, extending as far as 200 miles (322 kilometers) inland.

I fluttered my elytra, trembling in wonderment. I could scarcely imagine the vast stretches of time in which the land gradually rose, a few feet at a time, to such heights above the sea level.

One day, we were reminded that earthquakes were not the only forces that formed the magnificent landscapes of the South American coast. On this day, we walked to the base of the cliffs arising from the beach. We were leaning against the cliff, enjoying the fresh sea breeze and the warmth of the morning sun, when a pebble broke free from the cliff wall above us. Charles jumped aside just in time to avoid being hit on the head. The rock started a small avalanche, carrying a flurry of other small rocks along with it. We watched as they bounced along the sloping beach, breaking off a sharp corner here and there, finally coming to rest in a scattered pile on the sand.

"Rosie, look at the huge layer of gravel atop this cliff. It must have been formed by countless rock falls from an even higher, more ancient cliff!

"But how can that be? If the gravel layer were scraped into a mound in one place, it would form a great mountain chain!"

He was silent for a long while, his mind stupefied by the time needed to accumulate all of those pebbles, formed by masses of rock, falling piece by piece along old coastlines and riverbanks, rounded and tumbled as they were carried to their present resting place.

When we returned to the *Beagle,* Charles pulled from the shelf one of his favorite books, *The Principles of Geology* by Charles Lyell, a well-known English geologist whom Charles greatly admired. He wanted to see what Lyell had to say about the changes in the Earth's surface over time.

"Ah, here it is, Rosie," Charles exclaimed. "Lyell says that the mountains, valleys, cliffs, and shorelines we have been exploring must have been formed in the past the same way they are being formed now, by earthquakes, volcanoes, rock falls, and the constant motion of the sea."

I peered out from the porthole of the map room at the looming cliffs with their 50-foot (15-meter)-thick gravel covering. I thought of how the land had been gradually uplifted over a thousand feet by repeated earthquakes and volcanic forces. I considered the long, long history of the Earth and its ever-changing surface with a sense of deep wonder and awe.

That night I left another clue in Charles's journal.

March 1835 Chile

The land from the Rio Negro to Tierra del Fuego may have been lifted up by a series of earthquakes (like the one we witnessed here in Chile) over a vast span of time.

eight successive cliffs and plains extend into the continent

present beach

upraised beach

upraised plain

ocean

white limestone layer containing ancient plankton and sea shells

gravel layer containing ancient sea shells

red mud layer containing fossils of gigantic land animals.

The uprising movement has been interrupted by long periods of rest during which the sea ate deeply back into the land, forming the long lines of cliffs which separate the step-like plains.

Clue No. 6

The Earth changes over time, sometimes slowly and sometimes more rapidly. Many small changes accumulate over unimaginably long periods to alter dramatically the face of the Earth.

For the next several months, under the meticulous command of Captain FitzRoy, the crew charted the western coast of South America. In Lima, Peru, we spent seven weeks stocking the *Beagle* with provisions for the long trip back to England, by way of Tahiti, New Zealand, Australia, and Africa.

We left Peru on September 7, 1835, and arrived at our first stop on the way home—the Galápagos Islands—on September 17.

CHAPTER 7

The Galápagos Islands

Seeing this gradation and diversity of structure in one small, intimately related group of birds, one might really fancy that from an original paucity of birds in this archipelago, one species had been taken and modified for different ends.

Charles Darwin, The Voyage of the *Beagle*

Charles's broad shoulders sagged with disappointment when we landed on Chatham Island—one of the fourteen large islands in the group of islands called the Galápagos, off the coast of Ecuador.

"Nothing could be less inviting than this broken field of black lava, sparsely covered with stunted, half-dead brushwood," he groaned. But, although we did not realize it at the time, from here we would be led to one of the most important clues to the mystery of mysteries. We spent several weeks exploring the Galápagos Islands, which lie a few hundred miles off the western coast of the mainland.

The plants and animals we discovered here exist nowhere else on Earth. Even the giant tortoises, which swim from island to island and clamber upon the beaches to mate and lay their eggs, are found only in the Galápagos. Every island is unique: not only the tortoises, but also most of the insects, birds, and lizards found on each island are different from the ones found on any of the others. The cycle of life is played out under slightly different conditions on each island, in a slightly different way, by a singular cast of characters.

At the same time, the plants, insects, birds, and lizards all resemble each other, too, and they also look like those found on the distant mainland of South America.

Among the unique qualities of the Galápagos wildlife was their stupidity!

"Can you believe it, Rosie?" Charles wondered out loud. He had repeatedly thrown an iguana into a deep, wide tide pool. No matter how many times he threw it, the animal returned again and again to the place from which it had originally been thrown. "This fellow climbs out of the water as fast as it can, even though that's where it usually gets all its food. It keeps coming right back to me for another dunking. This creature is as stupid as it is ugly," he added.

Charles and I have quite different standards of beauty, but I had to agree with him about this particular iguana. Like others of his kind, he was both hideous and sluggish. Even his name was clumsy: *Amblyrhynchus* is not exactly music to the tympanic membrane.

"Could this fellow's contradictory behavior occur because it has no natural enemies on land?" Charles mused. "I wonder if it has a primitive sense that there is more danger in the water from predators such as sharks; but it has no instincts about dangers on the land. Perhaps it heads for land, no matter what emergency it meets. On balance, this would usually promise safety."

I wandered away to think about what Charles had said, and to look for relatives of my own. They were not easy to find, for most of them avoided the harsh sun beating down on the islands by doing their work at night. After a diligent search I met several. I found them to be a dull lot, but like the other living creatures of the Galápagos, they belong to unique groups found only here. I did have an amiable conversation with a busy individual named Sticky, short for her scientific name of *Gersteckeria*. She was enjoying a meal of cactus pads and moved aside for me to join her.

I appreciated my cousin's hospitality and determination to get her night's work done, but declined the meal. I was not disappointed that our stay in the Galápagos was short. I was dreaming about a real meal of tender rosebuds grown in green England.

We spent a little more than a month exploring the islands. Indeed, our time there was so rushed that Charles had very little time to examine his samples as thoroughly as he wished to. A number of finches were among the important birds that Charles collected from the islands, stuffed, and shipped back to England.

We left the Galápagos Islands and set out on the 3,200-mile (5,150-kilometer) voyage to Tahiti on October 20, 1835. We sailed under clear skies, urged onward by favorable winds, and reached that beautiful island by mid-November. We enjoyed the rushing waterfalls, friendly people, and forests of Tahiti, but when we left them behind on November 26, we felt only mildly sad, for with every day on the sea, we were drawing ever closer to our beloved England.

CHAPTER 8

Change Over Time

. . . These elaborately constructed forms, so different from each other, and dependent upon each other in so complex a manner, have all been produced by laws acting around us. . . . Thus, from the war of nature, from famine and death, the most exalted object which we are capable of conceiving, namely, the production of the higher animals, directly follows.

Charles Darwin, The Origin of Species

"What is that high-pitched, vibrating whistle?" Charles exclaimed. It was mid-December and summer in New Zealand. We were returning from a late-evening walk in a deep pine forest outside a village called Waimate. Our companion, a Christian missionary named the Reverend Williams, with whom we were lodging, immediately stood still, motioning for us to be quiet.

"It is the sound made by a wingless bird called the kiwi," he whispered, leaning forward to scan the forest path. We followed his gaze and saw a stout brown bird poking its long, curved beak into the ground in several places.

After the kiwi disappeared into the underbrush, Charles expressed his delight at having caught sight of the shy bird. "Wingless birds!" he marveled. "They resemble the flightless birds of other continents, like the ostrich, which use their wings not for flight, but like sails to take advantage of the wind and run faster."

"That does not seem possible," rejoined the Reverend Williams, "for the kiwi has no wings at all, really, only little stumps ending in tiny claws. And I doubt that the ostrich or any other bird has nostrils at the end of its beak, as the kiwi does."

"Nostrils at the end of its beak! I never heard of such a thing!" Charles shook his head back and forth at first, then began to nod instead. "I suppose nostrils would be very useful to a night-loving bird living on the ground in a dark forest. It would be able to smell its food, even in the dark."

That evening as he settled into the comfortable bed in the Reverend Williams's guest room, Charles murmured sleepily, "Wings have so many different uses. I have been thinking about the penguins of South America, which use their wings as fins; and of the steamer birds whose wings are used for paddling; as well as the flightless ostrich, which hoists its wings to catch the breeze; and of the great condors that soar high above the landscape searching for food. In each case, the shape of the wing reflects its use. For the kiwi, I suppose, which lives on the ground in the dense New Zealand forest, wings are of no use at all."

As he drifted off to sleep, he mumbled one last thought: "What if all birds started out with similar wings, but in each different environment, a wing form that was slightly more useful, perhaps because of stronger chest muscles, or a sleeker shape, was passed on for generation after generation? There would be only tiny, almost undetectable changes between one generation and the next. . . ." Soft snores followed, and I knew it was time to provide Charles with another clue to the mystery of mysteries.

December 1835 New Zealand

Change in form of wing over time? Each generation has wings slightly better suited to its distinct habits and environment.

Familiar form of wing for flight

New Zealand
The kiwi has no need for wings, living on ground in dense forest.

South America - the ostrich uses wings as sails

The penguin uses small wings like fins

How many generations must have passed to arrive at these extraordinary wing forms?

Clue No. 7
The most useful version of an inherited trait may be passed on from generation to generation. Over time, these small differences add up, so future generations may look very different from their ancestors.

In early April we reached the tropical Cocos Islands northwest of Australia. By this time it was clear that Charles had been thinking about how, in life as well as in geology, many small differences can make a big difference over time. While I nibbled on a piece of fresh coconut on the glistening white sands by the lagoon, Charles waded into the calm blue water for a closer look.

"Rosie, these islands are among the most wonderful objects in the world!" he called to me. "The huge living coral reef surrounding this island lagoon is built on a coral foundation. The whole structure rests on a sunken volcano more than a mile beneath the surface of the water, according to Captain FitzRoy. But corals are among the tiniest of animals with skeletons. Every particle of this island, and all the other islands around us, is made up of the minute bodies of living creatures. How many eons it must have taken!"

Charles and I were glad to have seen the beautiful tropical islands, but even such beauty could not compare with our homeland. Each day our thoughts turned toward England. But we still had almost half the globe to cross.

By May of 1836 we reached South Africa and spent two weeks there. Charles dutifully recorded his observations. We reached the Ascension Islands on July 19. One morning in mid-August, to our surprise and distress, we found ourselves heading on a west-southwest course toward Brazil, rather than north toward England. Captain FitzRoy had found a problem with his measurements and wanted to retrace the course we followed when sailing out of England. We made the best of the delay, and were able to walk one last time in Charles's beloved rain forest. Charles found it as beautiful as ever, in spite of his longing to be at home.

On August 17, we finally directed our course toward home. Stopping only briefly for supplies at the islands of Porto

Praya and the Azores off the coast of Portugal, we finally arrived in Falmouth, England, on October 2, 1836. The *Beagle* harbored there for a few days, then sailed on to Plymouth. Charles and I, unable to wait a moment longer than need be, took the mail coach to Charles's family home at Shrewsbury. Such a homecoming! I had several narrow escapes, almost being crushed in exuberant embraces as Charles's sisters, father, brother, cousins, aunts, uncles, and friends greeted their much-loved, long-lost traveler.

While he was away, Charles had become famous! His letters to Professor Henslow, and his carefully preserved specimens, shipped from ports along the voyage, had excited scientists all over England. Charles was welcomed as an important member of the scientific community.

Charles began to study his specimens and think about what they could tell him about the mystery of mysteries. One clue remained to be discovered, and that clue was revealed by the finches Charles had collected on the Galápagos Islands.

When we left the Galápagos, Charles had grouped them together for shipping, without noting which island some of them came from. Finally Charles and his colleague, John Gould, an expert on birds, had a chance to look at the finches that Charles had shipped home. "It is nothing short of marvelous how the beaks and other features of these birds suit them for the kinds of food available to them," Charles marveled.

"Yes," Mr. Gould pointed out, "where seeds are the main source of food, the finches have stout beaks designed to crack tough husks; but where the best food is wood-boring insects, the finches have long beaks they can use to probe beneath tree bark."

I watched as Charles tried to sort the birds according to their islands, lining up all of the birds by beak size, smallest to largest. He wanted to group them and give each group a distinct species name. "You cannot tell where one group ends and another begins!" he exclaimed in frustration. "The differences between birds that are next to each other when they are laid in a line are too slight."

Charles rearranged the birds again and again, trying to find a way to make clearly separated groups. "When you line them up, they grade into one another. But if you go along the line and choose birds that are farther away from each other in the row, you can see that the slight differences add up. Where can you draw the lines among the groups?"

One really has to think about this question for a while to realize how important it is, for it reveals a central and final clue to the mystery of mysteries.

December 1836 London

Finches collected on Galapagos Islands – can these specimens be sorted by beak size and shape so as to indicate which island each one came from?

Tree finches

insect eating

woodpecker like

vegetarian

Ground finches

seed eating

cactus eating

Clue No. 8

Even when two species are very different, there may be some individuals or groups that have traits that fall between the two extremes.

As the excitement of our return died down, Charles confided to me that he was ready for some peace, quiet, and the companionship and comfort of family life. He had fallen in love with his cousin, Emma Wedgwood. They married in January 1839 and soon moved to a quiet home in the country not far from London to raise their growing family. I loved Emma, and I believe the feeling was mutual, for it was she who supervised the planting of several fine rosebushes in the garden.

I continued to accompany Charles on long walks. We would reminisce about our adventures, and he continued to think about the mystery of mysteries. I listened and waited for him to figure it out, for he had all the clues he needed.

And so do you.

All the clues are listed together on the next two pages for you to think about. The following chapter holds the solution.

Rosie's Clues to the Mystery of Mysteries

1. Every living organism is unique. Individuals vary, even within the same species.

2. Living things have special traits that enable them to survive in their own particular surroundings. Within a species, some individuals may have a version of the trait that is more helpful to survival than other versions.

3. In any given environment, each living thing has a special role to play in the intricate cycle of life. In different places, similar functions in the cycle of life are carried on by different organisms.

4. The individuals that are best able to compete in the struggle for life pass on their survival abilities to their offspring. Individuals that are less able to compete often die before they have offspring. Soon, the only individuals left are those that have inherited the ability to compete most effectively for food or space or safety.

5. New species appear and old ones disappear as the Earth changes. Many of these extinct organisms resemble the ones now living in the same part of the world.

6. The Earth changes over time, sometimes slowly and sometimes more rapidly. Many small changes accumulate over unimaginably long periods to alter dramatically the face of the Earth.

7. The most useful version of an inherited trait may be passed on from generation to generation. Over time, these small differences add up, so future generations may look very different from their ancestors.

8. Even when two species are very different, there may be some individuals or groups that have traits that fall between the two extremes.

CHAPTER 9

The Solution

There is grandeur in this view of life, with its several powers, having been originally breathed by the Creator into a few forms or into one; and that, whilst this planet has gone cycling on according to the fixed law of gravity, from so simple a beginning endless forms most beautiful and most wonderful have been, and are being evolved.

Charles Darwin, The Origin of Species

Different kinds of living things are called species. For Charles Darwin, the mystery of mysteries included the following questions: Why are there so many different species of living things? Why are they so well adapted to their surroundings? Where do these species come from?

It took Darwin almost ten years after the voyage of the *Beagle* to figure out the answer, and it took him many more years of thinking and observing before he felt sure enough of his solution to share it publicly. Darwin called his solution "the theory of natural selection."

DARWIN'S SOLUTION TO THE MYSTERY OF MYSTERIES

The Theory of Natural Selection

Darwin's theory of natural selection is based on four main ideas:

Variation. In every species, there are differences among individuals that can be passed on from parent to child.

Adaptation. Depending on the environment at any given time, certain differences may help some individuals to survive better than others do. These helpful differences are called adaptations. Individuals with helpful adaptations will pass them on to their descendants. The proportion of individuals within the species that has the helpful trait increases. When this happens, we say that evolution has taken place within the species.

Descent. All species are related to each other in a huge family tree. Living species are the descendants of earlier parent species.

Change over time. The Earth is constantly changing. In any species, individuals who are better adapted to a new environment will tend to live longer and have more descendants. After a long period of time, the descendants may be so different from their ancestors that they are considered to be a new species. When this happens, we say that a new species has evolved.

Darwin's theory explains the evolution of new species. It works much like the process that dog or horse breeders use when they select the traits they want in future generations. Charles Darwin realized this, and so called his explanation of the mystery of mysteries—the evolution of new species—natural selection.

When many changes accumulate over time, the individuals in recent generations may be so different from those in the past that they represent a new species. The form of the new species reflects its adaptation over time to its own unique environment.

The clues also helped Darwin to understand why some species share more similarities than others. This is a result of how natural selection works through time and space: Sometimes groups within a single species may be separated by rivers or mountains. They may encounter different environments. As differences accumulate through time, groups that resembled each other at first may become very different because their environments require different qualities for success. Even so, each group may keep many of the qualities of the original species (like the resemblance among the giant extinct ground sloths and the present-day sloths of South America).

Species that have been separated by rivers, mountains, or other obstacles for a shorter period of time often continue to share many similarities (like the beaks of the Galápagos finches). Species that have been separated for a longer period of time may share fewer similarities.

Sometimes a similar way of life results in the selection of similar traits, even in organisms that have separated from a common ancestor long ago (like the fungus-loving beetles of South America and England).

Charles Darwin discovered that all the wonderful varieties of organisms living today are the descendants of one or a few original species. He found this view of life to be exciting, mysterious, and grand. Hopefully you do, too.

AFTERWORD

One Mystery Leads to Another

Long before having arrived at this part of my work, a crowd of difficulties will have occurred to the reader. Some of them are so grave that to this day I can never reflect on them without being staggered; but, to the best of my judgment, the greater number are only apparent, and those that are real are not, I think, fatal to my theory.

Charles Darwin, The Origin of Species

Although Rosie is a fictional character, Charles Darwin was real. The adventures described in *The Voyage of the Beetle* are true ones, recorded by Darwin in his notebooks and in a book he published in 1839 about his adventures, *Narrative of the Surveying Voyages of His Majesty's Ships* Adventure *and* Beagle *between the years 1826 and 1836 Describing their Examination of the Southern Shores of South America and the* Beagle's *Circumnavigation of the World* (later republished as *The Voyage of the* Beagle). The dialogues between Rosie and Charles, of course, never occurred. However, their conversations reflect the thought processes that led Darwin to natural selection theory, his explanation of the mystery of mysteries.

The other characters in the book are real as well. Captain FitzRoy; Jemmy Button and the other Fuegians; the cruel plantation owners; and the tall, handsome gauchos were all described by Darwin.

The comical incidents included in this book were chosen to show that Darwin was open to new experiences and able to laugh at himself. The nickname Gas, the nasty-tasting beetle, the challenges of sleeping in a hammock, the misery of seasickness, and the accident with the bolas were described in Darwin's journals and books.

Darwin and his wife, Emma, had ten children. Sadly, one daughter died in infancy and a little son died before his second birthday, shortly before Darwin's theory of natural selection was presented to the world at a meeting of the Linnaean Society in London. A third beloved child, Annie, died when she was ten. Darwin was a devoted husband and father, even when he became busy with his scientific work.

Throughout his life, Darwin continued to observe the natural world and to write about it. He made many friends among the important scientists of the time. In 1859 he published one of the most famous books of scientific theory, *The Origin of Species By Means of Natural Selection.* In this book he brought together his years of observations and thoughts about natural selection.

Not everyone agreed with Darwin's ideas. Many people tried to prove that he was wrong about natural selection. But in all the time since *The Origin of Species* was published, no one has been able to scientifically prove that the theory of natural selection is incorrect.

Charles Darwin changed the way we think about life on Earth, but he did not have all the answers. Since he introduced the idea of natural selection, we have learned about how traits are inherited through the transfer of genes from one generation to the next. We have found many, many fossils that show how one species has changed into another. And we have learned that some species change gradually over time, while others change more rapidly, depending on the challenges and opportunities they face, and their ability to adjust to changes in their environment.

But none of these discoveries would make sense without the enthusiastic curiosity, brilliant insight, hard work, and carefully recorded observations of Charles Darwin.

APPENDIX I

Timeline of *The Voyage of the Beetle* Following Darwin's Timeline in *The Voyage of the* Beagle

May 1831	Cambridge, England—Rosie meets Charles.
December 27, 1831	Devonport Naval Base, Plymouth, England—the H.M.S. *Beagle* sets sail.
December 30, 1831	Bay of Biscay—Charles gets seasick.
February 29 (Leap Year), 1832	Bahia, Brazil—Charles encounters the rain forest.
July 1832	The *Beagle* leaves Brazil, continues south, charting the coast along Uruguay and Argentina.
January 1833	Tierra del Fuego, Argentina—Jemmy Button, Fuegia Basket, and York Minster return to their homes.
March 1833	The *Beagle* visits the Falkland Islands.
April 1833	Charles and Rosie admire sea slugs in Patagonia, southern Argentina.
August 1833	Charles rides from the mouth of the Rio Negro to Bahia Blanca, Argentina. He finds fossils of huge, extinct mammals at Punta Alta.

June 1834	The *Beagle* sails through the Strait of Magellan.
February 1835	Charles and Rosie observe the devastation of an earthquake on the island of Quiriquina, off the coast of Chile.
March–September 1835	The *Beagle* continues to survey the South American coast, anchoring in Lima, Peru, for several weeks to stock up on provisions.
September 7, 1835	The *Beagle* leaves South America, beginning the yearlong journey back to England.
September 17, 1835	Charles and Rosie begin exploring the Galápagos Islands off the coast of Ecuador.
October 20, 1835	The *Beagle* leaves the Galápagos and sets sail for Tahiti, 3,200 miles (5,150 km) away.
November 15–26, 1835	Tahiti
December 19–30, 1835	New Zealand
January 12–March 14, 1836	Australia
April 1–12, 1836	Cocos Islands, NW of Australia
April 29–May 9, 1836	Mauritius

May 31–June 18, 1836	South Africa
July 8–14, 1836	Saint Helena, in the South Atlantic Ocean
July 19–23, 1836	Ascension, in the South Atlantic Ocean
August 1–5, 1836	Returns to Bahia, Brazil, to confirm earlier measurements.
August 12–17, 1836	Takes refuge from storm at Pernambuco, on the coast of northeastern Brazil.
August 31–September 4, 1836	Porto Praya
September 19–25, 1836	Azores
October 2, 1836	Charles and Rosie arrive in Falmouth and take a mail coach home to Shrewsbury (the *Beagle* itself returns to Plymouth and moves on to Greenwich, then to Woolwich).

APPENDIX 2

Timeline of Charles Darwin's Life

February 12, 1809	Charles Darwin is born in Shrewsbury, England.
1817	Charles's mother dies.
1817–1818	Charles is a student at Dr. Case's Unitarian day school.
1818–1825	Charles is a student at the Reverend Butler's boarding school at Shrewsbury.
1825–1827	Charles studies medicine at Edinburgh University; he cares little for medicine but loves natural history.
1828–1831	Charles studies religion at Cambridge University but is more interested in collecting beetles than in attending lectures. Charles meets his lifelong friend and mentor, Professor Henslow, who shares his love of natural history.
1831	Charles passes his final exams at Cambridge but stays on one more term to study geology.
1831–1836	Charles accompanies Captain Robert FitzRoy as the ship's naturalist on the H.M.S. *Beagle*.
1836–1839	Charles returns to England. He stays in London, organizing his collections and writing descriptions of them for scientific journals.

1839	Charles marries Emma Wedgwood; *Narrative of the Surveying Voyages of His Majesty's Ships* Adventure *and* Beagle *between the years 1826 and 1836* is published (later republished as *The Voyage of the* Beagle).
1842	Charles and Emma move to Downe, about 25 miles (40 km) from London.
1844	Charles writes a short article about the idea of natural selection.
1842–1858	Charles continues to experiment, observe, and write. He and Emma have ten children, three of whom die in childhood.
1858	Charles and Alfred Russel Wallace, who also traveled around the world as a naturalist, present their ideas about natural selection to the Linnaean Society of London.
1859	*The Origin of Species,* destined to become one of the most important scientific books ever written, is published.
1859–1882	Charles continues to investigate and write about the life of worms, orchids, climbing plants, and many other organisms, building up evidence in support of the theory of natural selection. April 19, 1882, Charles dies. A week later he is buried at Westminster Abbey near the tomb of Sir Isaac Newton.

GLOSSARY

ADAPTATION The process by which an organism develops traits to take advantage of its environment. Some organisms, especially animals, do this by learning. Other traits are not learned; they are inherited.

ANCESTOR An earlier member in a line of descent (e.g., a parent, grandparent, or great-grandparent).

BAROMETER An instrument for measuring air pressure, used to determine altitude or predict changes in the weather.

BRIG A sailing ship with two masts, each rigged with a square sail.

CARNIVOROUS Meat eating.

CORAL A colony of small marine animals whose hard skeletons mass together to form an elevated ridge on the seafloor.

DESCENDANT A later member in a line of descent; an organism related to another organism that lived in the past.

ELYTRA The hard outer covering wings of a beetle; also wing cases.

ESTUARY The mouth of a river along a coast where freshwater mingles with salt water.

EVOLUTION A process of continuous change in the characteristics of groups of organisms throughout generations.

EXTINCT A group of organisms that has ceased to exist.

FOSSIL The remains or traces of an animal or plant that have been preserved under the surface of the Earth.

FUNGUS (*PL.* FUNGI) A living organism (e.g., mushrooms) that reproduces by spores, has no chlorophyll, and obtains nutrients directly from other organisms.

GAUCHO A South American cowboy.

GEOLOGICAL FEATURES Features of the Earth's surface (mountains, rivers, cliffs, volcanoes, and valleys) that are formed over time by natural processes.

GEOLOGIST A scientist who studies rocks, minerals, the structure of the Earth, and the natural forces that shape it.

GUN ROOM Quarters of the midshipmen and junior officers on a ship. On a ship such as the *Beagle,* the "guns" are actually cannons. Pistols and rifles, which are portable, are called "small arms."

INHERITED Passed on from parent to offspring.

INSTINCT Behavior that is not learned, but is inherited from one's ancestors.

LAGOON A shallow body of water formed behind a barrier of coral. Lagoon islands are often circular in shape, with a coral wall surrounding a quiet inner lake.

LARVA (*PL.* LARVAE) The immature, wingless stage of an insect's life.

MANDIOCA A tropical plant with a fleshy, edible root; sometimes called manioc or cassava.

MAYORDOMO A Spanish term for the manager of a hacienda, ranch, estate, or village.

METAMORPHOSIS Transformation from an immature insect to an adult.

NATURALIST A person who studies nature, especially living things.

NATURAL SELECTION Process by which traits that help an organism survive are passed on to its descendants. Organisms that do not have these helpful traits may be less successful at survival or have fewer successful offspring. Eventually, most of the members of the group have the helpful traits, and many of the unhelpful traits are lost.

ODIOUS Hateful.

ORGANISM A living individual; may be a bacterium, protozoan, fungus, plant, or animal.

PALEONTOLOGIST A scientist who studies fossils.

PARISH A church community.

PLANKTON A mass of tiny plants and animals that float near the surface of a body of water.

PREY Animals that are hunted by other animals for food.

REEF An ocean ridge made up of minerals and the skeletons of living coral, built on a foundation of dead coral.

SPECIES Groups of organisms that tend to look alike and have the ability to reproduce together.

STERN The rear part of a ship.

THEOLOGY The study of religion, especially the Christian religion.

THORAX The middle segment of an insect's body, between the head and the abdomen.

TRAIT Feature or characteristic of an organism.

TYMPANIC MEMBRANE Thin layer or tissue stretched across an opening that transmits sound vibration. In humans this is the eardrum; in beetles, it is a membrane on the abdomen.

WING CASES *See* elytra.

BIBLIOGRAPHY

Barlow, Nora, ed. *The Autobiography of Charles Darwin 1809–1882.* New York: Norton, 1993.

Darwin, Charles. *The Origin of Species.* New York: Gramercy Books, 1998.

Darwin, Charles. *The Voyage of the* Beagle. New York: P. F. Collier & Son, 1909–1914.

Keynes, Richard Darwin. *Charles Darwin's* Beagle *Diary.* Cambridge, England, and New York: Cambridge University Press, 1988.

Leff, David. AboutDarwin.com: A Web site dedicated to the life of Charles Darwin. Available at www.aboutdarwin.com. Updated February 12, 2007.

Stone, Irving. *The Origin: A Biographical Novel of Charles Darwin.* Garden City, NY: Doubleday, 1988.

Zahradnik, Jiri. *The Illustrated Book of Insects.* Secaucus, NJ: Chartwell Books, 1991.

FURTHER READING

Books

TO LEARN MORE ABOUT CHARLES DARWIN
AND THE VOYAGE OF THE *BEAGLE*:

Altman, Linda Jacobs. *Mr. Darwin's Voyage.* Parsippany, NJ: Dillon Press, 1995.

Anderson, Margaret J. *Charles Darwin, Naturalist.* Berkeley Heights, NJ: Enslow Publishers, 1994.

Darwin, Charles. *The Voyage of the* Beagle. Amherst, NY: Prometheus Books, 2000.

Twist, Clint. *Charles Darwin: On the Trail of Evolution.* Austin, TX: Raintree Steck-Vaughn, 1994.

TO LEARN MORE ABOUT INSECTS:

Evans, Arthur V., and Charles L. Bellamy. *An Inordinate Fondness for Beetles.* New York: Henry Holt and Company, 1996.

Zahradnik, Jiri. *The Illustrated Book of Insects.* Secaucus, NJ: Chartwell Books, 1991.

TO LEARN MORE ABOUT THE RAIN FOREST:

Albert, Toni. *The Remarkable Rainforest: An Active-Learning Book For Kids.* Mechanicsburg, PA: Trickle Creek Books, 1996.

Berger, Melvin, and Gilda Berger. *Does It Always Rain in the Rain Forest? Questions and Answers about Tropical Rain Forests.* New York: Scholastic Reference, 2002.

Sayre, April Pulley. *Tropical Rainforest.* Brookfield, CT: Twenty-First Century Books, 1994.

TO LEARN MORE ABOUT
JEMMY BUTTON AND THE FUEGIANS:

Hazlewood, Nick. *Savage: The Life and Times of Jemmy Button.* New York: Thomas Dunne Books/St. Martin's Press, 2001.

TO LEARN MORE ABOUT NINETEENTH-CENTURY VOYAGES OF EXPLORATION:

Williams, J. E. D. *From Sails to Satellites: The Origin and Development of Navigational Science.* Oxford; New York: Oxford University Press, 1992.

TO LEARN MORE ABOUT FOSSILS:

Lindsay, William. *Prehistoric Life.* New York: Knopf, 1994.

Osborne, Roger, and Donald Tarling, eds. *The Historical Atlas of the Earth: A Visual Exploration of the Earth's Physical Past.* New York: Henry Holt, 1996.

Parker, Steve, and Jane Parker. *Collecting Fossils: Hold Prehistory in the Palm of your Hand.* New York: Sterling, 1997.

Spinar, Zdenek V., and Zdenek Burian (ill.). *Life before Man,* revised edition. New York: Thames and Hudson, 1995.

The Visual Dictionary of Prehistoric Life. London; New York: Dorling Kindersley, 1995.

TO LEARN MORE ABOUT GEOLOGY:

Downs, Sandra. *Shaping the Earth: Erosion.* Brookfield, CT: Twenty-First Century Books, 2000.

Hooper, Meredith, and Christopher Coady (ill.). *The Pebble in My Pocket: A History of Our Earth.* New York: Viking Children's Books, 1999.

TO LEARN MORE ABOUT NATURAL SELECTION AND EVOLUTION:

Creagh, Carson. *Things with Wings.* Alexandria, VA: Time-Life Books, 1996.

Facklam, Margery. *And Then There Was One: The Mysteries of Extinction.* New York: Little, Brown, & Company, 1993.

Silverstein, Alvin, Virginia Silverstein, and Laura Silverstein Nunn. *Evolution.* Brookfield, CT: Twenty-First Century Books, 1998.

Web Sites

AboutDarwin.com
www.aboutdarwin.com

This is an excellent site that features a clear, day-to-day description of the *Beagle*'s voyage, along with beautifully detailed maps. It also includes a timeline of Darwin's life and work, as well as plenty of biographical information and links to other Web sites.

Destination: Galápagos Islands
www.pbs.org/safarchive/galapagos.html

This Web site includes a cyber field trip to these beautiful islands.

How the Kiwi Lost His Wings
www.destination-nz.com/page.php?x=content/kiwiwings.html

A Maori tale about the Kiwi

Online Literature Library—Charles Darwin
www.literature.org/authors/darwin-charles/

This Web site contains the full text from Darwin's books: *The Voyage of the* Beagle, *The Origin of Species,* and *The Descent of Man.*

Transitional Vertebrate Fossils FAQ
www.talkorigins.org/faq/faq-transitional.html

This Web site lists transitional fossils for many groups of animals.

INDEX